CURIOSITY SAVES CAT

Aundrea Veney

ADVAS Oasis Inc.

ISBN-979-8-9918486-0-2 eBook
ISBN-979-8-9918486-1-9 Paperback

Cover design by: AI ChatGPT Agent
Printed in the United States of America

CONTENTS

INTRODUCTION

As our world transitions with time so does the views, experiences and beliefs of ourselves and children we raise. Circumstances we may find ourselves in are not necessarily to prevent us from growing but rather thrusting us into a wider mindset. This book was written with the intent to encourage readers to be open when confronted with differences, fearless when challenges arise and most important, curious about life and the unpredictable surprises it holds. We all can learn something new that can enhance not just our lives but the lives of those we come in contact with every day.

Curiosity Saves Cat
Aundrea Veney

CHAPTER I.
ANTICIPATION

The action of anticipating something; expectation or prediction
"her eyes sparkled with anticipation"

"Last call, last call to line up", Mrs. Johnson yelled amongst a large room of graduating high school seniors.

I cannot believe we are really about to do this. Where the heck is Cat? I don't see her anywhere. I know we are not supposed to have our cell phones but I'm going to call her to make sure she is ok. Just as I get ready to dial, she runs up to me out of breath.

"OMG where have you been you almost didn't make it", I say.

"I know, I know, the reverend had a prayer breakfast this morning and that ran over".

"Seriously, they couldn't have rescheduled knowing today was your graduation day".

"You know how they are. Cat said looking timid".

Let me give you a little background story of Cat and I. Cat is my best friend and has been since we were nine years old. Everything about our lives says we shouldn't be friends but here we are eight years and two-family deployments later. Her parents are still married, her dad is chief master sergeant in the air force, plus he is a pastor at an evangelical Baptist church. She was raised in a very conservative manor. No pants, no makeup, no music outside of gospel, no boyfriends, no sex before marriage and a host of other no's that lead to the biggest problem in my opinion. NO real idea who she is.

Me on the other hand, my dad is gay and was kicked out of the military because someone saw him at a gay bar and that's not allowed in the military. Since then he has started his own government contracting firm that has done pretty good so far. My dad raised me to explore life and anything that interest me with as little limitations as possible. He always says, "what and who you were created to be will find its way to you". I love him for saying that because please believe I have used those words as my mantra to get out of trouble whenever he is upset with something I did. What can I say, I'm an eternal explorer of life.

Both Cats dad and mine were in the air force together which is how we met. I'm an only child and Cat is the youngest of six children. Her mother is like a character out of a 1950s history book of good housewives. My mother left for good after coming to terms with my dad being gay. See how similar our lives are... But as far as I can see it there is no rule book on who should and should not be friends for life.

It seems just like yesterday Cat and I were screaming at each other from one end of the cul-de-sac to the other because we were on punishment and could not leave our front yard. Now look at us, all grown up and ready to graduate high school. Cat's plans after graduation consist of her going to Spellman College in Georgia. She received a full academic scholarship so why not go. As for me, I plan to serve our country in the air force just like my dad did before they kicked him to the curb. I want to travel and see the world, while gaining master skills to be a leading professional in the corporate industry when its time... well at least that's what the commercial said.

Dear God can our school choir sound any worse?! I could hear the painful sounds of their voices belting out our school song echoing in the tunnel where we all were lined up ready to walk out to the stadium in front of our friends, family, teachers and other peers.

"Lexi!!" Cat yelled.

"You're in the wrong spot, go get in your line".

I didn't even realize I was standing in the M line when my last name started with D.

The stadium is packed; I wish I would have gotten a pair of goggles to see where my dad and Shane, his boyfriend, was.

"Lexi, Lexi, look", Cat yelled. "Look at the banner in the stands" as she pointed to the front left of the stands.

Well I'll be. Cat's family had a huge neon green banner with both our names on it in pink. My dad and Shane were there too screaming and cheering for us as we made our way to our seats. Quick side bar, Shane is dad's partner. I never thought he would settle down after mom left but as he says Shane is his soul mate; I'm happy that he's happy. Aww they are so cute. Aside from the slight embarrassment, I'm glad I didn't have to wonder where they were anymore.

"Cat, did you tell them to do that?" I asked. At this point our classmates were obviously annoyed we kept talking to each other over everyone as if were not on opposite ends of the floor.

"I had no idea, she said. You know I would have given you a heads up".

I guess she has a point. As the program started and the national anthem concluded we all sat anxiously waiting for the only reason we were even here, to get that paper baby! The whole senior class started a petition to get Jim Cary to speak at our graduation but instead we were blessed with our very own. Mr. Dooney, the school principal. I believe he lives for moments in the spotlight with the microphone. Somehow he thinks he is some kind of Tony Robbins in the making. Suddenly all the lights went out, darkness filled the stadium, some didn't know if they should run for the closest exit or sit and brace themselves for the next terrorist attack, then music starts and laser lights seem to be dancing to the beat….

"Are you serious?" I say out loud. Smoke ascends from the stage and out walks Mr. Damion Dooney. What the heck is wrong with this man! Standing on the stage looking like a washed-up rapper; just who does he think he is?!

"Ladies and gents, boys and girls; people all over the world. We are here to celebrate theze here GRAD-U- ATES!!! Oh yeahhhhh!!"

Wow, I do hope his wife is somewhere wearing a disguise. Now the moment we have been waiting for; the presentation of the diplomas. It seems like they take forever to call my name. When they do I freeze!

"Lexi, go!" Everyone was yelling at me as I held up the line for others to have their moment too.

"Oh Oh Oh Okay", I responded. Too bad I didn't make it look as graceful as Cat had done walking across the stage, shaking the hand of the dean with her right hand while accepting her diploma with the other hand. I will never live my moment down. I tripped walking and almost broke my ankle because it was the greatest idea I ever had to wear 5-inch heels, something I have never done before in front of thousands of people with cameras. I also forgot to grab my diploma after shaking the deans' hand and walked away, only to realize and run back and get it. This messed up the spotlight and photo op of my next classmate. I'm sure his parents won't mind seeing both of us in his picture accepting his diploma. Boy, am I glad this day is over. Please just bring on the food and after party since that was all I could think about.

CHAPTER II.
DISPIRITED

Having lost enthusiasm and hope; disheartened.
*"she was determined to appear unworried in
front of her dispirited family"*

"Lexi I won't be able to come to the graduation party", Cat says with tears in her eyes.

"What do you mean Cat, this OUR party, my dad did all of the planning for both of us! We have over 100 people RSVP'd to come and NOW you're telling me you can't come?! Who does that?!" I know everyone within a five-mile radius heard me because I was just that furious.

"I know, I know and believe me I tried but it was not changing my parents mind" Cat said.

"Well why not?!" I asked.

"Lexi, please don't, you know why".

"Are you kidding me Cat!"

"It's not me!", she yelled, "it's my parents you know this". She said.

"Damn it Cat whatever, go run home to the good reverend and Martha Steward, I'm over it! I pray one day your dad and mom are dying and are in need of an organ transplant and the only one that can help is a flaming queen of a gay man or better yet a transgender".

"Lexi don't be like that; look I will see if I can talk to my mom later on alone and she may change her mind once she knows how important this it to me and you. Okay?".

"Okay", I respond begrudgingly.

"Bless your heart and soul", Cat says as she leans into my forehead.

"Bless your soul and heart" as I lean back towards her placing our hands on each other's heart. That was a special thing we had been saying and doing since the night Cat tried to kill herself in elementary school. After many months of what I consider the perfect mother storm of stress for a six-grade kid. Dealing with serious home issues, then being bullied and harassed at school by other students and teachers, it's a miracle she survived it.

You see Cat has long hair and as some would say had the body of an eighteen-year-old girl. She always wore church clothes to school because her parents didn't allow her or her siblings to wear anything else. Not to mention she was really pretty, so secretly I think other girls were jealous of her. As if that wasn't bad enough she refused to tell her parents because she said they never do anything to protect her. I honestly don't blame her.

The spring of our fifth-grade year, her parents left to go on a romantic vacation, and instead of some random babysitter, they had her uncle fly in from Boston, to watch over all six of her brothers and sisters. While they were gone her uncle locked the two of them in the laundry room and did unthinkable things to her while her older siblings were still at school. He told her if she told anyone he would make sure no one believed her.

I don't know how effective that was at the time because she came to my house, hysterically shaking, and crying while telling my dad and I everything. She was too scared to go back home and sleep anywhere and feel safe. My dad was furious and allowed her to stay but confronted her uncle the next day. In turn things got so heated between the two. Cats uncle threatened to call the military police (we call them the MPs) and tell them he was gay if he didn't mind his business. He obviously had a habit of making threats to people; however, this was a hard situation for my dad. Ultimately, he conceded but insisted Cat stay with us until her parents returned and that was it.

Cat saw how everything played out and felt helpless. My dad tried to reassure Cat that she was safe at our house and always welcomed, while also explaining the difficult spot he was in if he reported anything. He offered an alternative by telling Cat if she personally told her parents or the MPs we would be there to hold her hand and back her story to make sure his actions would not go unpunished. It just couldn't be initiated by my dad.

Cat didn't really seem sold on the idea, so instead she counter offered an alternative to his idea and that was, she would write a letter and tell her parents when they came back and let them take care of it. I know I'm not the smartest cookie in the jar but that just didn't seem like the best option but then again who was I to say, Cat was going through it not me. My dad didn't seem too sold on the idea either but if she was sure, and he asked.

"Cat, are you sure about this?"

Several times, then he said he supported that decision and of course I did too.

"We are in this together", I said giving a group hug. She stayed with us for the rest of the time her uncle was there and when her parents came back, she went home for one night. I assume she gave them the letter because the next night her mom called my dad and asked if it would be okay for Cat to stay with us for the rest of the spring break through the summer. My dad agreed

"Flexi Lexi, you need to put fresh linen on the guest bed we have company staying for the next few month".

Of course, I responded in only a way a pre-teen could... "what you talking about dad".

He responds. "Cat is going to be staying with us for the rest of the school year through the summer".

"Are you serious, are you really serious" I squealed.

"Yes, so get to it".

No more than two hours later Cat shows up to my house; it was the best reunion ever. I always love having her around, she was like the sister I never had. We woke up every morning together, fought over the bathroom, went to school together, did our homework together, it was amazing. We always got along; she always loved to stay up listening to music and watching music videos; she was never allowed to watch or listen to at her house. We would have dance parties and prank call people on the phone all night, sneak out the house and double dare each other to run in the street with just our panties and bra on.

We spent summer days at the beach or the mall running up dad's credit card, and in the evening, we would often go to the drive-in movie theater with dad, and binge out with pizza, Reece Peanut Butter Cups, Twizzlers and soda. That was the best summer ever.

CHAPTER III. SNOOP

Investigate or look around furtively in an attempt
to find out something, especially information
about someone's private affairs.
"your sister might find the ring if she goes snooping around"

It was now the end of summer, Cats uncle had left and everyone was preparing to go back to school. I really felt sad Cat had to return home but we still spent the same amount of time together except overnights. Returning to school this year was extra special because we were the seniors of elementary school… everyone looked up to the six graders, so we had a reputation to uphold.

Cat and I made sure we wore similar outfits for the first day of school. We both had our hair down, with white shirts and jean skirts and a jean jacket with princess Rebooks sneakers. My dad dropped us off, so we wouldn't have to take the school bus the first day; that made our grand entrance even better. We walk in school and it seemed like all eyes were on us.

I will admit Cat did have more confidence this year than she did before. I think all that shopping, dancing and carefree stuff we did all summer that her parents would call acts of the devil, allowed her to feel like she fit in a little more, instead of being blocked off from all normal human interactions outside of church like she had always been prior to. It was also good therapy to help her forget the god-awful thing her uncle had done. Anyway, we owned it and the girls that were jealous before were extra jealous now, it felt amazing. With all the first day madness, Cat and I sat next to each other at lunch and talked about this new guy who started school which for some reason all the other girls seemed to have already called dibs on.

I thought he was pretty hot, but Cat didn't seem remotely interested in him. It was all the better because that would be really weird for us to have to flip a coin to see who could try and get his attention. Needless to say, I tried and the only thing he seemed to want to talk to me about was Cat... which was cool because it wasn't like I was shopping around for a husband. When the word spread that he only had eyes for Cat, which again Cat was not feeling the same in return, the other girls became even more upset, as if the rector of "being upset" could get any higher. They started this smear campaign against her in a matter of weeks. I watched as this beautiful confident person I knew as my best friend was getting the joyful high spirit snuffed right out of her. I got into a few fights defending her from the stupid posters someone placed all over the school saying she was a slore (slut + whore) or rumors started saying she had sex with her brothers' high school football team.

It was sad, not to mention, some of the teachers started treating her like she was the problem student, since most of her classes would end with someone going to detention even though she was a straight A student. All of this because of a boy and girls thinking it was Cats fault they couldn't get him!! It made me sick.

I told my dad to do something about it and he told me he would talk with the principal. About a week after that things calmed down a little and then Cat starts to get really sick every morning.

"Lexi". Cat whispers on the school bus.

"What's wrong?" I ask.

"I just don't know I can't hold anything down and I feel tired all the time. My mom said she thinks it's the stomach flu but she and the reverend prayed over me but this time it's not going away. I really think I am dying".

"Cat, you're not dying, stop being silly. Maybe it's because you just are not sleeping enough. You know you get sick every year after your parents have their revival and church convocation.

I don't know why any parent would keep their kids out at church until 2am and expect them to make good grades and function at school. I mean really, what in the world could anyone be doing at church THAT LONG? Are you hand making the instruments for the band to play and the pews to sit on before you all even start service". I laugh out afterwards.

"No Lexi seriously".

Cat didn't even chuckle at my joke as she usually does.

"I think God is going to take me".

"Shut up Cat, we will just go to the nurse when we get to school".

"Okay", Cat said as she put her head on my lap.

I feel pretty bad for her at this point. When we get to the school we get permission from our teachers to go to the nurse's office and it wasn't hard because Cat left part of her guts on the floor of Ms. Silverman's classroom. It smelled awful.

"Somebody clean up on aisle one!!" I said laughing as I helped Cat walk down the hall. I get excited for moments I am able to avoid doing any class work.

When we get to the nurses office she helped Cat back to the bed and told me I could leave but Cat asked if I could stay and she allowed me. After asking Cat a hundred and fifty questions and not seeming satisfied with any of them, she then asked Cat if she had started her cycle yet. Cat answered, yes, which by the way was so unfair because I didn't even start mine yet and Cat did. She always seemed to get the womanly things before me. First it was the scary hair, then boobs, then her period. What's next?!

"Well maybe it's your hormones", the nurse said as if she had an epiphany.

"Why would that make me sick though?" Cat asked.

The nurse further explains "for some girls when they are on their cycle the hormones can be so much, your body is just trying to process all the changes, so feeling nauseous, having headaches, losing your appetite, and feeling tired are all things that can come from PMS or being on your cycle. Good news is I can give you medicine for that".

"Really?!" Cat said in such a hopeful voice. "You mean I really am not going to die?"

"No silly" the nurse said. "You will be fine. Now when was your last period?" She follows up.

"Hmm that is a good question: Cat said. "Lexi you tell her; you keep track of that stuff better than I do".

"Aww man Cat, I actually stopped counting since before the summer".

"That is weird because I don't think I came on since before the summer… is that even possible?" Cat asked under her breath.

"Well how about last month", the nurse interrupted trying to ease Cats busy mind. "You don't need the exact day but maybe the beginning, middle or end of the month. Can you tell me that?"

Cat seemed to have gone into a trance

"Cat, do you know?" I asked

"It wasn't last month maim!" She said as tears poured down her face.

"Okay well that's alright; you don't need to cry about it. Just to be on the safe side, you're not sexually active, are you?" The nurse said very reluctantly.

"No maim I'm not, I'm a ……." Cat paused for a minute…" no, no I'm not sexually active".

"Ms. Smith she isn't having sex, are you kidding, look at Cat. Do you ever see her with any guys around here like some of the other girls?" I said as a matter of fact. "No point intended Cat, it's not a bad thing, but you understand what I'm saying right?" Trying to pull my foot out of my mouth, since Cat was looking at me as if to wonder how I could say such a thing…

"Okay I understand but I have to ask. Lets' do this; go in the bathroom and pee in this cup and I will be right back". Ms. Smith said.

Cat said okay and when she got out of the bathroom, she and I sat on the bed trying to recall the last time she did have her period. Between both of our minds, we were able to pinpoint the time when her uncle was there and raped her. Before we could even talk about it in detail, the nurse came back in.

"Hi ladies sorry to keep you waiting I needed to run across the street to the Rite Aid real fast. Where is the cup?" She asked.

We both pointed towards the bathroom. When she came out she had a stick in her hand and held it up shaking her head. Cat and I both looked puzzled. In the bottom of my stomach I knew something wasn't right. Ms. Smith pulled up a chair and asked Cat if she wanted me to leave for the conversation she was about to have with her.

Cat said "no, Lexi stays for whatever this is. She stays!".

Ms. Smith said "okay" as she held Cats hand in one hand while holding the stick in the other hand. "Sweetie you are pregnant", she said in the most loving voice.

At that point all I could hear was my heartbeat, and it seemed like time just slowed down. I was looking at Cat and it seemed like her lips were moving in slow motion while her voice sounded like she was underwater. Did this lady just say that? Am I dreaming? How is this going to affect our lives? How in the world will we tell her parents and my dad? Internally I'm screaming – JESUS, TAKE THE WHEEL OR ME INSTEAD!!!

"What do you mean?" Cat replied… "this can't be true… Lexi, did you hear her…. Are you serious?"

I snap out of my trance. "Cat, just take a deep breath".

We both locked eyes and knew exactly when it happened and who did this to her… we both started crying.

Ms. Smith comments… "if you're not sexually active, you have to explain to me how you have managed to become pregnant".

I had a feeling Ms. Smith knew it was more to the story than we were willing to share.

Cat immediately said... "I'm sorry, I lied I do have sex and I am sorry for lying, I just didn't think anyone would ever find out"

Wait, what is going on? I know Cat doesn't have sex. I am with this girl all of the time and we both KNOW it was her uncle, so why is she telling Ms. Smith this.

"Please don't tell my parents, I promise I will tell them, it just can't come from you okay". Cat said to Ms. Smith in a sense of desperation.

"Okay Cat but I will be following up with you in about a week to make sure you told your parents. Okay?"

"Yes maim, thank you". She said. "Lexi help me up please".

"No, you can rest here for a little, but I will get you some crackers and ginger ale to take away the sick feeling. No need to rush back to class, you have a lot to process. "Lexi would you like some too", she asked.

"Yes please". I need something I thought. If it can't be a miracle to save Cat I guess I will have to settle for a soda and crackers too. Just as Ms. Smith opens the door to leave we see Stacy and Kimberly sitting outside of the door. Those were the same girls who started the smear campaign against Cat.

"Ohh no Lexi did you see them; do you think they heard us. OMG what if they tell everyone, what if this gets out"

"Cat, deep breaths; deep breaths I say. Don't worry about it. They didn't hear anything, I'm sure. They are just being their normal creepy selves". I try extra hard to reassure Cat. About an hour passes and after conversations about how she was going to tell her mom and if she needed me or my dad there, to us coming up with a plan to keep the baby and have her move in with me and my dad while she was home schooled. We came up with quite an elaborate plan but until that could be enforced we decided we needed to go back to class. Today was a half day so we didn't have much time left in school to finish up anyway. Finally, the last bell and then we were headed to the school bus for a destressing weekend. As Cat and I got on the bus right before it pulls off, we see creepy Stacy and Kimberly standing on the sidewalk facing our bus, yelling and waving…

"Congratulations on the baby Cat… we knew you were a slore!".

All eyes on the bus turn and look at Cat. I knew Cat was going to have a meltdown so the only thing I could do was deflect with information that was more believable…

"Stacy, stop trying to make people forget you got caught going down on the janitor in the science lab after school last week".

Laughter erupts. I don't think the kids knew what to believe but either way I knew this was not good that the two school mouths almighty did in fact hear everything that was going on with Cat.

"Lexi, why would you lie like that," Cat asked.

"Look I had to do something to get the attention off of you because you are not good at hiding things".

"Thanks"… she said as a tear dropped down one eye.

"Everything is going to be okay Cat, I promise".

CHAPTER IV.
INDIFFERENT

Having no particular interest or sympathy; unconcerned.
"they all seemed indifferent rather than angry"

Well, the weekend was finally upon us. Fortunately, this was another weekend Cats parents were going to be away and were allowing their kids to stay with friends so they could keep their marriage fire hot, as they always said. I tell you, if anyone ever thinks preachers or old church people don't get it on, I can assure you they do. Cat's parents are always stoking their fires away somewhere. No wonder they have six kids. Someone should put an extinguisher on those things before someone gets hurt.

Anyway, this means Cat was back at my house for the weekend which made things even better. Now she will have much more time to just relax and not think about anything but fun. Dad had already made reservations for movies and things were off to a great start. When Cat arrived she still seemed down but within a couple of hours between the sugar and music I had her back in carefree land.

We went out to dinner, saw a scary movie with Dad and Tony, had ice-cream after and then did our regular prank calls before bedtime. For some reason tonight Cat was taking forever in the bathroom. I knocked on the door four times and no response. Maybe she fell asleep taking a bath, I mean she was trying to destress right. I told my dad after an additional five minutes, so he could give a try at knocking and when she didn't answer he became concerned so he broke in the bathroom.

That night in my bathroom we found her on the floor, lifeless, next to an empty bottle of bleach and an empty pill bottle. What did she do? It freaked me out! My dad who saved her life by rushing her to the hospital so quickly, the doctor said. Her parents were contacted, and when they arrived my dad tried to explain everything that could have possibly caused her to try and take her life. Her dad refused to believe anything he said and rather accused my dad of trying to molest Cat. He said my dad probably drugged her up as an attempt to keep her quiet while he had his way with her.

"After all everyone knows you don't get enough female action these days" he blurted out.

I was so shocked the reverend would even think such a thing, let alone say them. All I could do was sit paralyzed speechless. My heart hurt in a way I never knew was possible. My father always taught me to respect my elders and always show love to others including strangers but Im not feeling very loving or respectful to this man I thought I knew. How could he say that to my dad? I mean really, this is the man that has allowed your daughter to stay at our house while he made other things a priority over her. Do people really think my dad is some sex crazed maniac, trying to prey on kids just because he loves differently than they do? Has his life and actions not shown how awesome of a man he is? As tears formed in my eyes a doctor came around the corner.

Mr. Daniels. Mr. McKinney.. he calls.
Yes doctor as both of them raced over to see what he was going to say. Cats mom and I stood back in the family waiting area trying to listen and read the doctors lips from afar. It seemed like he said something like she got here just in time... blah blah serious trauma...blah blah I couldn't make out the rest. Maybe I should have wiped my eyes a little more.

Lexi! My dad called for me.

Yes dad.

Come quick he replied.

Of course I moved as quickly as my 5 feet legs would take me.

Cat is asking for only you, so the doctor says you have about 5 minutes before she has to rest for the night.

Ohh Okay, I said nervously. I have never seen anyone in the hospital in real life. Can someone show me where her room is? I asked.

Sure! The doctor replied, I will take you back, follow me.
And I did. When I got back to Cat, I had to hold it together because she had tubes coming out of her nose, arms and private! Seeing it on Greys Anatomy is one thing but real life is a whole other thing all together. I just imagined I was Dr. Meredith Grey and I walked over to Cat and grabbed her hand like they do all the time on the show. I think they call it bedside manors or something; clearly it worked because she looked up at me and smiled. A sense of relief came over me.

Hey, what's the deal pickle? I asked.
As she tried to sit up and whisper, everything's kosher.
I told her not to do too much and save her energy.
She whispered again... I guess I don't have to tell my parents now.
I knew exactly what she was talking about.
We both looked at each other and all I could think of was what she must have been feeling to think killing herself and the baby would make it better. She looked back at me, almost with eyes that were trying to explain and plead for help at the same time. We sat in silence for a whole 5 minutes. The doctor came in to tell me it was time to go because she needed her rest. All I could say out of my mouth as I put my forehead on hers since it was the only tube free zone on her body, was bless your heart and soul Cat.
She squeezed the hand that was already holding hers and pulled it

to her heart and mumbled back; bless your soul and heart.

I laughed and told her, thanks but she had the words wrong. I didn't say that.

She chuckled and whispered.. Oh well. It sounded better the way I said it.

That was the night we continued to use those words and those gestures to say everything to each other that didn't need to be said out loud. For some reason even in the midst of the hospital machines, the tubes, the doctors, our parents fighting in the other room and the serious issues that got her here in the first place we knew everything was going to be ok.

We left the hospital that night and my dad starts in with a random speech in the car drive home about how we have to make sure we don't keep secrets from each other and if anything bad happened to me that I can feel safe to let him know no matter what it was. I responded with daddy I know. I was getting a sense that either he too knew about the baby now or that he was just making sure I didn't end up like Cat. Then he proceeds to explained that an investigation was going to be initiated because of the report he provided to the hospital on the events that lead to us finding Cat in the bathroom. Of course that included the story about Cats uncle. I asked very concerned. Well dad what is that going to do to your career and what will happen to Cat when her family finds out, and what will happen to me if they try and take you away?

Whoa, take it easy kiddo, he said in his calming voice. It's fine, I will be fine, Cat will be fine, you will be fine, we ALL will be fine. You don't worry your beautiful mind about it.

He always had a way to make you feel that everything was already worked out even if it wasn't.

CHAPTER V.
ELABORATE

Involving many carefully arranged parts or details;
detailed and complicated in design and planning
"Elaborate security precautions"

L exi!! Lexi!!! Did you change your clothes yet? My dad is yelling down the hall.

Yes dad; I just don't know if it's the right thing to wear. Cat and I were planning to wear matching outfits since this is our graduation party but now that she may not be coming I don't know if I should put on another outfit. I yell back. I hear his footsteps coming closer to the door.

Lexi, you're beautiful just like that, so stop stressing. He says in that calming tone.

Besides at the end of the night I am sure you will be out of those clothes and in your swimsuit anyway, Shane chimes in.

We all burst out laughing.

They always know how to calm my explosive rants.

Okay well lets go get ready to party! I scream.

The house looks amazing, my dad and Shane really outdid themselves this time. There are white and gold balloons all over the place with the perfect mix of blue tulips, roses, lilies and hibiscus flower arrangement strategically placed throughout the inside and outside. I see a huge white tent that drapes our backyard with lights adorning the tops and sides of the tent and iron yard fence. Candles short and tall, light the walk ways leading to the pool, where additional floating candles, gracefully dance on the waves of the pool water. Lights at the bottom of the pool make the water seem crystal blue. Inside the tent is a huge glass looking dance floor with clear matching tables and chairs with blue and gold linen and chair bows. The smells of smoked bar-b-q and spiced rotisserie lamb fill the air. I am sure everyone in the community has watering mouths thinking about partaking in this amazing feast we are about to chow down on.

While all of this looks good I don't see my crab cakes that dad knows is my favorite. All I know is they better make an appearance before this party ends. There are several people walking around in black uniforms attending to every detail. My dad would be please to know they are on it, even when he isn't around. We have had parties here before but none of them even come close to this. If I didn't know any better, I would think they are trying to make this look like the wedding they will never have, let my dad tell it.

Oh wow! They have the cotton candy machine, Cat, and I asked for, then to the left the dunk tank and inflatable obstacle course we desperately begged for. I can't believe this is really happening. I have to call Cat and at least give her a visual of what's going on, I'm sure she would appreciate that.

Ring, ring, ring, ring... gee it sure is taking her a long time to answer. Her voice mail didn't even pick up yet. Just as I get ready to hang up.

Hello.. Cat answers on the other end of the phone.

Cat!!, what are you doing? I ask, not really wanting a response.

Im about to ….she starts.

You have got to see this Cat, I interrupt her. I am going to video call you so you can see this okay? So answer! I hung up before she could say anything in response.

Ring, ring... she picks up and accepts the video feature on the call. Good! I say, with excitement. Cat, check this out. I turn the phone to pan across the inside of the living room, then outside to the deck in the backyard to the tent and around so she could see the dunk tank, grilling stations and inflatable course. Ohh look at the dance floor Cat!! All of this is for us and its amazing right? I ask.

WOW Lexi, OMG that is amazing did they do all of that without your help? She asked.

Girl you know I didn't lift one finger. Dad and Shane hired some people to take care of it. They wanted to do a big reveal for us but since you were not here they just let me see it before all the guest start to come. Speaking of guest did you know they have some special entertainment for us? I can't wait to see what or who it is.

It all sounds amazing Lexi, Cat says. Well I really hope I can get there to enjoy it with you because it looks like a celebration of the century is about to go down.

I know right…

Then an awkward silence came over the phone as we looked at each other through our android phones.

Lexi, I need to go now…

I know, I know I didn't want to bother you but I just wanted to share this with you in case you don't make it. Bless your heart and soul;

Bless your soul and heart and then we hung up.

CHAPTER VI.
HAUGHTY

Arrogantly superior and disdainful.
"a look of haughty disdain"

A few days after all the drama at the hospital from Cat's attempted suicide Cats mom knocked on our door. I was the only one home at the time and I knew Tony, would be there shortly and then my dad not long after him.

I am sure your wondering who Tony is; well his full name is Anthony. He and dad met on a trip in Italy. Dad doesn't seem to be as into him as he is into my dad; don't know what that's about but I'm sure his days are numbered. In the mean time I will enjoy him spoiling me trying to win my dad over.

I answer the door very curious.

Hi Mrs. McKinney, is everything okay? I asked looking around in case her crazy husband or brother in law was hiding in the bushes..

Lexi, of course it is. Is your dad home? she asked in her Stanford wives tone.

Nope he sure isn't. What's up? I asked because at this point I'm feeling like this lady has some nerve and a lot of explaining to do.

Well, can I come in and wait for him she asked.

I quickly responded. Well of course, my dad won't be here for another 30 minutes, but Tony should be here before him if you need to speak with an adult. I knew that would make her skin crawl and hopefully go away but it didn't oddly enough. She looked at me, shook her head.

Lexi Lexi- you are something else as she pushed me to the side and walked in. Of course I don't mind, I can wait, even Jesus sat amongst the gentiles so who am I to do any different...

This lady is just as crazy as her husband.

Fine then! .. Well me casa es su casa, would you like anything to drink?

Yes please, thanks Lexi.. She responded. It's something about the way she says my name that makes me want to be called Sue or something with one syllable to limit the time I have to hear her voice.

Do you have any fresh lemonade?

Well I scooped the freshly stored powder from the can and made that like an hour ago so it should be cold by now, want some?

Hmmm no, it's okay do you have bottled water?

Sure do, I said.

Well alrighty, let's have that.

As she sat down I ask, how is Cat? Just for small talk because I obviously know already seeing her every day at the hospital...

Ohh she is blessed by the lord; was her reply.

Yeah okay.. Awkward silence entered the room.

SIDE DOOR OPEN, the alarm speaks to let me know someone was coming in. Tony walks in around the corner.

Flexi Lexi, how's it going kiddo? Holding an extra smoothie with my name on it

Tony!!! Hi, you shouldn't have. As I grab the strawberry banana kiwi cup of loving smoothieness. We have company, I say with a mouth full of cold smoothie. Its Cats mom; she dropped by;

Mrs. McKinney Tony, Tony Mrs. McKinney....

She stands and extends only her hand to shake..

Oh dear how are you, bring it in Tony says as he throws his muscular arms around her. It must be so hard with your baby girl being in the hospital.

She tried really hard to escape his embrace but it was pointless, it was no escaping the bear hug of Tony.

It's quite a challenge, she tried to fix her clothes back to their normally stiff nature, but nothing the good lord won't bring us through, she says.

Please, please sit, take a load off Tony says. Well you should know we love Cat, just like she is our own and we keep you all in our prayers.

Yes I am sure. She says.

GARAGE DOOR OPEN. The alarm tells me. I know THAT was my dad.

Dad I yell; Mrs. McKinney is here; we're in the living room. Dad not as warm as Tony had been, Kisses me on the forehead, gives Tony a head nod and looks at Cats mom.

Elizabeth. He says.

Timothy, she says in return.

Tim, please he replies. What brings you over?

Well as you know Cat is scheduled to be released from the hospital in a couple of days, she says rubbing her hands as though she just put on lotion. .. And with the investigation going on, CPS has informed us Cat will be the custody of the state until the investigation is done unless we have other family or guardians who can claim her.. sooo.. I was thinking she says in the shakiest voice. Since Cat and Lexi are best friends and I mean... they go to the same school... and as her voice fades and eye contact disconnects with my dad.

I mean you have obviously done a good job with Lexi by yourself and you did save Cats life. . So despite your sinful life choices... as her previously lost confidence reappears..

All be it who am I to judge. You seem to be a decent human being, would you mind being Cats guardian until this whole thing blows over?

The room goes silent. My dad responds. I'm sorry can you repeat that because you lost me on the corner of compliment and insult.

Oh sweet lord let's not make this a big deal. Mrs. McKinney says. Can you temporarily take care of my daughter like your own.. Yes or no?

My dad burst out laughing and I could tell that he was super offended and I was afraid he was going to say no just off of principal being as though the McKinney's never hid how repulsed they were by my father and how hell bound he was for living such a perverted and sinful life is exactly how they explained it. I mean really I can't say I would blame him after the reverend pulled that stunt at the hospital. All I could do was take a deep breath and hope my dad could feel my heart and hear my thoughts.

"Daddy please please please please with cherry on top let Cat come stay with us." You could feel the tension in the room and the silence that lasted all of 5 seconds felt like an eternity as Mrs. McKinney impatiently said in a hasty done... so will you do it or no?

Daddy looked at me, then looked over at a picture on the mantel of me and my mom, as he put his hands on his hips like I have seen all the military men do with the last three fingers tucked into the pocket while the pointer fingers and thumb rested on his waist. Then he looked out the window as if someone was standing there telling him the answer. Yes, Yes I will do it. Cat is always welcomed here, he says.

Whoo hoooo I yelled jumping for joy, Cat is coming, YES!!

Now settle down Lexi, he said. Mrs. McKinney and I need to take care of some other things.

Mrs. McKinney interrupted, what other things, you said you would keep her what else is there, sweet baby Jesus do you want us to pay you too?! Are you trying to extort money from us? Oh Lord, I should have known.

Elizabeth! What?! Are you kidding me? My dad responded.

Don't nobody want your money lady. We just need to make sure all things are taken care of legally. I need an official agreement drafted and signed by you and your husband stating you are giving me the rights to act as legal guardian over Cat so no one comes back and says I tried to abduct her or hold her against her will and your knowledge.

Well that sounds reasonable. Mrs. McKinney responds. We will have that done by close of business tomorrow since this is a time sensitive matter.

Sounds perfect, wouldn't you agree Lexi? My dad looks in my direction and winks.

Just perfect!

CHAPTER VII.
IMPASSIVE

Not feeling or showing emotion.
"impassive passersby ignore the performers"

With everything that happened to Cat, of course news traveled to school and everyone was asking me about her. It's funny how many stories were formed though; I heard she was kidnapped, she got married and moved away, she was having her father's child, oh and she actually died. I mean wowzers. Did people really think about some of that stuff, before they decided to share it or ask me about it I mean come on people! Either way they couldn't believe one story over another until I confirmed it so it was up to me to make sure no part of the truth was believed.

Creepy Stacy and Kimberly somehow felt it was them that triggered Cats attempted suicide but I wouldn't give them the satisfaction. Whenever I would see them in the halls I would make my conversations somehow centered on how Cat never tried to commit suicide but she was out traveling all over Europe for a missionary trip. I would bring in post cards from trips my dad went on just to throw everyone off even more. Stacy and Kimberly were second guessing what they knew to be the truth at the end of it all which meant my job was working.

CHAPTER VIII.
INTRIGUED

Arouse the curiosity or interest of; fascinate.
"I was intrigued by your question"

I t's hard to believe that in less than one month, dad and I will be leaving for Japan. He received his orders and this time I will be able to go with him. At first we were worried that I would be forced to stay with a relative here in the states while he left but it worked out that I can go with him. My dad said something about it being in my best interest to remain with him after all the trauma with him and moms' divorce and the lack of stability my mom had or something like that. I really don't care as long as I'm with my dad. Wow Japan, all I know about those people are that they cook a mean stir fry.

I absolutely love going to the Japanese Hibachi Steak Restaurants; my dining goal is to catch both the chicken and shrimp in my mouth when the chef tosses it at me as part of the entertainment. When I broke the news to Cat she wasn't happy at all; she is not really the emotional type but she cried immediately. Even though we know as military dependents or some would call us "brats" every two to three years we have to pack up and leave, deep down we figured it would pass us if we didn't plan for it this time. I will miss her so much.

Speaking of the devil....

Lexi, did you read what those people eat over there in Japan? Cat asked as she walked in my house heading straight for the kitchen.

What are you talking about Cat, those people you are talking about are called Japanese and they eat the same things we do. Haven't you been to the Shatakii restaurant? Dad and I go all the time.

No Lexi that's just what they want you to believe to get you there. I read they eat fried spiders, snails, octopus and animals we have as pets like cats and dogs!! Are you really telling me you are fine with this?

Not sure what Cat had for lunch and what book she has decided to indulge in but clearly it has her on some kind of nutty paranoia.

Cat it will be fine, as I laugh out loud, I couldn't hold it in.

Even if they do eat that stuff I'm sure it will be a subway or KFC somewhere for us to eat regular food if all else fails. I mean how bad can it be? We will be on a military base and I KNOW the generals and captains are not trying to work on insects, ocean rodents, and man's best friends most importantly their whole deployment. That's just ridiculous. I'm looking forward to; seeing how they dress, what music they listen to, and how they live; come on Cat we have to start focusing on the bright side of things.

(Six weeks later)

While walking in the streets of Okinawa I can say I was pleasantly surprised, the adjustment hasn't been too bad. There are a lot of America families, from the military base no doubt but the Japanese teenagers seem to be very westernized. The new school I attend has all the same types of clicks that they had in America.

The athletes all still hang together, the science geeks, the girlie girls who do nothing but look cute and then you have the artsy clan. The only difference is the artsy group here is like REALLY into the arts. Instead of hearing lines from a Shakespeare play being rehearsed in the halls or at lunch; you hear and see music beat creation collaborations being made on their computers with the occasional singer/rapper and dancer to compliment the sounds. It's very impressive. If I could dance, sing or make beats I would have to indulge. Like I said the kids here are not really any different than the kids back home.

The cafeteria ladies all seem to have the same universal attitude; the teachers all desperately want the students to really care about their lessons. Homework and test are always an unnecessary task that only makes since to the school boards and people reading reports that compare us to other schools.

The latest and greatest news is that I have found a new love interest. No, he is not Japanese, although nothing is wrong with that kind of thing, but my dad calls it puppy love. This puppy love was discovered with a big dog in school. His name is Jerome and he plays basketball. I don't even like the athletic type because they seem to always know they are hotter than the cat's meow, usually if you find a basketball player not far behind him is a long list of girls he is playing that all feel like they are the one.

Jerome and I kind of organically smashed into each other. By that I mean we were in the organic market five minutes from my house and while walking I bumped into him and smashed my Mizu Shingen Mochi on him; that name is a Water Cake; a popular dessert around here. I was so upset with the fact that I waited in the line for two hours to try this dessert just to have it smashed into nothing by some dumb tall human being who didn't move out of my way. I didn't notice how easy on the eyes he was or how apologetic he seemed to be at that moment.

By the time I accepted the fact that my dessert wasn't coming back, I could finally hear the words coming out of his mouth and saw he had the most amazing eyes. He was offering to make it up by getting me ice cream from some place uptown. Since I spent my last yen, of course I agreed. On the long walk, and trolley ride uptown I learned that he attended the same school I did and his family was stationed on the same base as me. This was the beginning of our beautiful love story. He was really like my customized prince charming. My dad liked him and his family liked me, what more could a girl ask for.

CHAPTER IX. ILLICIT

Forbidden by law, rules, or custom.
"Illicit drugs"

So it's been one full year since Lexi and her dad left for Japan. School has shockingly leveled out after being removed from the hot topics of our school tabloids. You can always count on sex scandals in high school. Some student is always rumored to be sleeping with some teacher or some girl was found in the boy's locker room or for us the latest and greatest, two art teachers were caught having sex in the school lavatory. It has been pretty hard for them to be taken seriously in their classrooms now but as long as no one is focused on me I really don't care.

It's funny as luck would have it my two school torturers; Stacy and Kimberly both have babies. It seems karma has a way of taking care of people. Motherhood seems to have aged them ten years ahead of their time. It's like they have joined the soccer's mom association before their kids even started walking. I kind of feel bad for them but I make sure I speak to them in the halls just to rub a little salt in their wounds.

I face time chat Lexi almost every day, which is really hard because of our time difference but we get in about 15 minutes of catch up time and that helps me feel like she is right down the street again. Our last conversation I let her know that my dad now received his orders to Germany. Lexi seemed excited and confused as she tried to figure out how the time would affect our video talks.

Hey Cat, what are you going to do about the food? She asked me in a mocking manor.

Whatever Lexi, Germany is nothing like Japan so be quiet. I honestly can't wait to see the Holocaust museums I have so many books about it and I feel like it's important to visit.

My parents on the other hand don't feel like it has anything to do with us so they won't be taking me. It's okay because I looked up the tours for the military families and they offer transportation for free. You see, where there is a will there is a way.

Cat you lost me at museums, what are you doing for the weekend.

I will be packing because we are scheduled to leave in two weeks.

TWO WEEKS?! Lexi yelled.

Yes Lexi. aww man our time is up.

We will catch up soon Im sure.

I will give you more details in an email so check it in an hour.

(Three weeks later)

Who would have ever thought that such a beautiful place would have such snobby people? I really don't like this place and I can't wait to leave. Whose idea was it anyway.. oh I forgot the stupid military; or might I say that grand ol Uncle Sam. Someone needs to start letting the wife of the grand uncle, chime in on where people should go. I mean everyone loves auntie's right. My school is actually a private school; under normal circumstances we could never afford anything like this but the country provides scholarships for the US military families so they get a good quality education while we are stationed here. I was telling Lexi that I haven't really met anyone and since the school is a specialty robotics school I spend most of my time studying just to keep up with my classmates.

As far as having a social life, that is not going to happen aside from the regular church activities my parents without fail have seem to find even in this foreign land. On that note the church we go to is multicultural. Instead of the regular Baptist style order of service they mix it up. One evening the priest started with something that sounded like a Hebrew prayer, and then it turned into praise and worship service with Filipino praise dancers and ended with a white man giving a sermon that sounded like Dr. Martin Luther

King Jr. It is never a dull moment. The only person at the church that has turned into a friend is this girl named Latavia. She is Japanese and Black and the first thing she said to me when we met at a community service event was,

Is that your hair? Would you ever get a boob job?

I thought it was odd but I never thought anything of it. People sometimes think we are sisters. I guess I could see how that is possible. For weeks we spent so much time together our families had finally got to the point we didn't have to ask to be over each other's homes. One evening at bible study I just so happen to be in the bathroom face timing Lexi trying to avoid my group bible lesson I didn't prepare for when I kept hearing these weird noised in the hall. I tell Lexi I needed to go in fear that one of the evangelist would catch me on my phone instead of talking with god in group like I should have been.

After we hang up, I slowly walk over to the door and crack it open just to make sure no one was there. As I walk out, I seemed to be walking closer to the sounds I previously heard. Subtle moans and groans is what I heard; just then I turn the corner and see Latavia being held by one of the elders of the church against the wall having sex. I instinctively wanted to run, scream and beat him off of her until she turned her head and seemingly looked like she was enjoying it. Our eyes locked, or might I say she caught me looking and motioned for me to be quiet and go away. I was very confused and didn't know what to think.

All of these emotions of what happened to me with my uncle came rushing back. I think I almost had an anxiety attack that very moment. After I snapped out of it I returned back to the bible class that finally seemed like it was concluding but not before Sister Myers asked me to recite my memory verse for the week. This woman was so annoying didn't she realize I was gone the whole class because I didn't study, now I'm obviously upset and stressed from what I just witnessed geesh can she give me a break with the stupid memory verse already!!

Sister Myers, I am really not feeling good, is there any way you can have mercy on me and give me a pass this week and I promise I will make up for it next week.

She looks at me as if she wanted to scold me and respond... I guess so Cat, I will however have to inform your parents.

Okay, I say, sighing relieved.

Just then Latavia walks up as if nothing ever happened in the last 20 minutes. She was now on Sister Myers' radar.

Ohh look who decided to join us at the very end of class. Little Ms. Latavia, class let's all stand while she closes us out with a wonderful benediction.

Latavia shockingly responds more pleasant than I.

Of course, Sister Myers, everyone, let us hold hands, and bow our heads.

She proceeds keeping it short and sweet.

"A child saved, is a soul saved, plus a life Amen".

Everyone said amen and we dismiss.

Latavia. I call her in a soft concerning voice

She looks over at me and waves for me to come quick.

Are you okay? What was that all about? I immediately ask.

Its fine Cat, just chill; that preacher pays me five hundred dollars just to do what his wife won't do I guess, or something, who cares though, we have money for shopping now.

Are you serious?! So you mean to tell me you like doing that kind of thing? I ask praying that she would somehow say no and that she was forced so she just makes the best of it however that was not the case.

Heck yeah I do! The way I see it is, I'm getting practice for my husband later on, and money for me right now. See, it's a win win.

I couldn't believe what I was hearing but there was nothing I could do.

Promise me Cat you won't say anything. If something like this got out, I will be ruined and in this country, I have heard girls get sentenced to death so please, she pleaded.

Sure, you don't have to worry about me saying anything. I promise!

That was the end of that and we said nothing else about it. I did find hanging around her to be very therapeutic on some levels. It was as though she used the life she was living as a source of empowerment or something. She didn't let it destroy her outwardly but then again who really knows what she is feeling on the inside.

CHAPTER X. SANGUINE

Optimistic or positive, especially in an
apparently bad or difficult situation.
"he is sanguine about prospects for the global economy"

L exi, can you go open the door?
I have no idea why my dad is yelling for me to do what he has hired help to do on my night. I dare talk back though, since he did all of this for me tonight.

That man could tell me to go catch a chicken and pluck it so they can cook it and I will do just that, you hear me! As I walk to the door, I realize it was just two of my classmates, so I open the door, graciously take my gifts and show them to the rest of the crowd.

At this time someone strikes up the karaoke machine and there was no way I was not going to show them how it was done. After Jason got off the floor from totally remixing Sir Mix A lot, Big Butts; I que the DJ to start my jam..... Love is A Battlefield by Pat Benatar.

We are young.

Heartache to heartache we stand.

No promises no demands, love is a battlefield...

I start singing as only I can and another voice joins me

Whoa, we are strong,

No one can tell us we are wrong....

Were my eyes deceiving me? OMG OMG CAT!!! Immediately I squealed and dropped the mic to run to her.

Are you serious right now? I asked. I can't believe you're really here Cat!

She is laughing with me.

I mean what did your parents say? What did you say? What did you do to get them to let you come? I flooded her with questions.

Lexi, I told you, my mom understood and let me go as soon as the reverend left for his men's meeting. Now let's finish celebrating because I don't have all night. I feel like Cinderella needing to get back before the strike of midnight but instead of my chariot turning into a pumpkin, my dad will find out I'm not home and will lock me away like Rapunzel in the dungeon never to see the light of day again.

We both laughed and resumed our karaoke song; everyone cheered now that the second honoree had arrived and the duo was back together. The food kept coming, as well as the guest; before 11pm even hit, it had turned into one of the biggest parties I had ever seen. Kids were bouncing on the bouncy house, splashing around in the pool, dancing to the music and eating until their hearts were content. No cops were called and no complaints filed. This was in fact a successful graduation party if I may say so myself. Cat and I deserve it. Who knows how long it will be before we see each other again.

CHAPTER XI. VEILED

Partially conceal, disguise, or obscure.
"a thinly veiled threat"

T he long road trip to Georgia was nothing but pure torture, thank god for music and headphones. I think my mother is a little emotional because she kept asking if we wanted wet wipes and Twizzlers. I don't know how the two go together but she made it. My dad on the other hand couldn't get me out of the car fast enough.
Let's go Cat, let's go!!!

The campus looked just like it did in the manuals, but what I wasn't expecting was all the loud music and creepy looking guys that were all lined up across the street looking at us, as though they were preparing to make a bid at an auction.

Stay focused girl, you came here for an education and that is what you better get, you hear me. My dad exclaims.

Yes, dad I know and the sooner we can get me settled the faster you all can leave me to get this great education. Little did he know I had absolutely no interest in those creepers.

The welcoming signs made things real easy for us to get to our next destination. For me it was the dorms first and the student foreign ambassadors' office second. I needed to get my schedule for the study abroad program I was enrolled in. Most schools allow the students to go during the summer or one semester starting their sophomore year but we were able to get into a program that allowed me to go after I completed my required freshman orientation courses. This means I will be flying friendly skis in two months. I really wish I could show Lexi everything. I know she would be so happy and cheering me on.

(Two months later)

Finally, I am done with my classes and leaving for India in three days. I didn't really expect to feel nervous because of how eager I was to get here but I am starting to really rethink this whole plan. I mean who goes to India to study abroad? What if I can't adjust? What if the people don't like me and they treat me bad?

So many thoughts start to run through my mind, but I guess it's too late to back out now. My parents would be so furious. I can hear them now; Cat you got a full scholarship and the opportunity of a lifetime to study in a place some only dream of going and now you want to back out because you don't feel good about it! Okay okay, after hearing that imaginary thrashing from my parents I get back to reality. It won't be so bad Cat, it's just a plane ride away and we are still on earth. It's not like it will be aliens or anything right. Let's do this.

CHAPTER XII. LAUD

Praise (a person or their achievements) highly,
especially in a public context.
"the obituary lauded him as a great statesman and soldier"

"ATTENTION". Tech Sargent yelled standing at our barracks doorway.

Everyone scattered like ants to their assigned bed post and stood tall and stiff as boards in the "attention stance" that was taught our first night in boot camp. Tech Sargent walked down the aisle inspecting uniforms and beds just as promised. As she made her way down the row, I could hear people getting yelled at for missing the mark, either the bed sheet was missing, the distance from the top of the bed to where they folded the sheet was off, or their uniform was not ironed.

One thing after the other; I, on the other hand was waiting eagerly to be inspected. To me this was like a regular Saturday morning in my house. Dad always gave me a timer to clean my room, shower and be dressed. After which time he would come in and inspect with a white glove, it's all I ever knew so this was like a cake walk for me. For some of my friends growing up they never understood it but now I am thanking my dad every morning I wake up in this place. For once I guess he did know something I didn't.

Airman Daniels, are you ready for inspection? She yelled.

Can I say I still don't for the life of me understand why they always have to yell right in your face as if you can't hear them. I'm pretty sure all of us had to pass a hearing test before we came in so unless those results didn't get passed down to this lady in here today, I would like to say this is completely uncalled for.

Maim, Yes Maim. I responded just as loud as she spoke to me, only to make sure she heard me loud and clear.

Let me be the judge of that Daniels, she says as she walks around my bed looking closely at every fold and tuck. She then pulls out a measuring stick.

Really lady? I thought. Is it that serious? She then drops to the floor looking under my bed for what I don't know, then she crawls over to my feet and looks at my boots as if she dropped her earring back between my laces. Whoa it's confirmed, this one fell off the looney train and I'm sure they are still looking for her because she needs to go back.

Daniels did you polish your boots? she asked.

Maim, yes maim…

I see that Daniels.

She makes her way up to her feet while her face was still extremely close to my body as if she was substituting for her German Shepard's job.

Did you starch your uniform too Daniels?

Maim, Yes Maim. I responded trying really hard to keep my facial expressions in check.

I see that Daniels. She yells. Squadron I want you all to gather around Airman Daniels right now.

Everyone huddles around me as if I'm in the middle of a rain dance circle or something.

This right here is who you all need to watch and imitate. I don't know what gutter some of you all were pulled out of the way you have become so comfortable with living in filth but this one right here got some learning from somebody and this is the result of it.

I'm almost in shock at what I'm hearing from the colonels' mouth. I don't know if I should smile or keep a straight face with my chin up.

She takes pride in the way she lives and looks. Her uniform is spotless, her bed and floor is spotless. You want to know what I was looking for under her bed? She asked, not pausing long enough for anyone to respond.

Well, it was dust, I was looking for dust and you know what you sorry sacks of crap.. I didn't see one speck of dust under her bed!! What that tells me is that this person standing in front of you pays attention to detail so I can count on her having my back on land, see or air. Watch, listen and learn from her. You all have 30 minutes to be little mini Daniels, I will return at 0600.

She leaves our room with her minions behind her, now everyone is looking at me as if I'm the problem child.

Don't blame me because I was born from a pool of amazingness.

Ironically it was only one other girl who actually came and asked me how I ironed my uniform and made my bed. I willingly shared the information and watched the others try to figure out what I had done without asking one question from me. I also now understand what my dad meant when he would say "Lexi, it's a sad set of affairs when you have a life jacket but refuse to use it". Dad always had these sayings that at the time seemed like blabber old man talk but it's all starting to make sense. Oh well, to each his own. I didn't come here to teach anyone anything anyway. I just want to earn my stripes so I can become a pilot.

CHAPTER XIII.
ASCERTAIN

Find (something) out for certain; make sure of.
"an attempt to ascertain the cause of the accident"

N O one could have ever prepared me for this. Yes, it's really different with all of the tons of people crowded in the streets, the colors, the noise and the smell is one you could never forget. But the energy and spirit of the people is just overwhelmingly loving.

When I landed, the daughter of my host family was there to greet me. Even though she was just 15 years old it somehow felt like we knew each other for years. She reminded me of Lexi, of course there is no way I could tell Lexi that, she would have a fit. Lexi always says "there is only one me, which cannot be duplicated".

Mansharup, that was her name, walked us to her home where I met her parents and her older sister Undyn who not only was beautiful but had a mysterious energy about her that I found intriguing. Everyone was so welcoming I don't think I could have asked for a better host family to be with. I video called my parents to let them know I was alive and was in good hands. My mom couldn't stop crying and my brothers and sisters were asking nonstop questions that I didn't have time to answer so I didn't.

Okay guys, I have to go, love you very much, go back to sleep. I said as I hung up.

I noticed Undyn was standing behind me in the doorway.

Hey, so are you the hanging out type or the book worm type? If you're the hang out type, do you want to go hang out? she asked.

She spoke really good English and that alone was impressive.

Well, I do read a lot but I'm always up for hanging out, so of course! I said.

Do I need to wear something in particular.

No, you're fine just as you are she responded.

Okay well let's go. I grabbed my passport just as I learned to do in the seminars in school. Never leave without your passport the words that kept ringing in my head from my professor.

We rode bicycles about ten minutes down the road when she pulled into this park.

You can put your bike here, she motioned.

When I finally locked my bike into the bike station

She asked, have you ever been to an active monk temple?

No, I respond.

Well good she says because we are going to an inactive monk's temple, so you have nothing to compare it to.

We both started laughing. I didn't care; all of this was so new to me I was like a child learning how to walk. I was eager, scared and yet very open to take in all I could in the short time I was here. As we walked along this beautiful path, that adorned a seemingly endless tranquil lake, we talked and laughed and shared things about growing up. I don't know why it was so easy to talk with her; we just had a very unusual connection. She told me about having a brother who was killed and how her parents use the hosting to try and fill the void of one less child in the home. Then she told me about her ambitions to be a basketball player and represent her country in the Olympics.

I told her about growing up with a strict family and how much we moved around and what it was like to be the new kid all the time. Then explaining how we were forbidden to have friends who were not of our faith. I told her about Lexi. She told me about music she liked, which oddly enough was country music, who would've ever thought. She joked about me loving pop and gospel and every other kind of music. She explained how conservative her country still is and that she watches a lot of American shows on her computer. Just as we got carried away yapping about our personal stories our walk ended at this breathtaking building that looked run down and abandoned. It stopped me in my tracks.

See this is the inactive temple. Undyn said softly. Long ago this was a monk's temple but with all of the construction and increased tourism they moved to another location that the public cannot go to. No one wanted to touch this because it is believed to still have healing powers and they say if you sit still long enough you can transcend.

What are you talking about Undyn I say chuckling.

I don't know, I am just telling you what was told to me she responded. Do you want to go look inside? She asked

Absolutely!

I follow her and as we both make sure we step carefully not to fall on the broken stone. We finally reach the inside that does have an amazing presence about it. Nothing I could ever put into words, but I stood looking over this massive valley that the temple shadowed over. You could see the perfect reflections of sun that kissed the lakes water, which reflected the trees that seem to stretch to the horizon. I have never seen anything more beautiful in all my life, I said.

I know exactly how you feel Undyn said.

As I turned to look at her, she was looking right in my direction instead of at the breathtaking view.

Uhm are we talking about the same thing I responded.

She quickly changed the subject and asked me to tell her more about Lexi. There isn't really much more I can say about Lexi except that aside from being my best friend she is my rock.

Tell me more she said… Well, it's a long story.

We have time, she responded.

For some reason I found myself telling her things that I had never told anyone outside of Lexi and it felt so natural. How is this even possible I kept thinking in the back of my mind? We talked for hours sharing the most traumatic and most intimate things two people could share, leaving them completely vulnerable but it felt safe. For the rest of my time in India we would meet back at the abandoned temple several times a week. Just to spend time with each other. I would tell her all the new things I learned about her country and the work I would have to do for school, and she would tell me about her job and how she was progressing with basketball training. The last week there Undyn asked if we could meet a little later than we normally did because she had something planned. I agreed and couldn't wait to see what it was.

By the time I started walking up the lakes path I noticed there were red lantern lights that lead all the way up to the temple I could not believe it. Did Undyn do this or did she trick me into some kind of cult ceremony. I arrive at the temples entrance and there are candles all over with colorful blankets and pillows for us to sit.

WOW you did this just for me? I asked.

Yes Cat, I wanted you to have something to remember me by. Come sit she said.

Good because I was hungry, is that the food over there, I pointed to boxes that were in a crate.

Yes, Cat but we are not eating yet.

I gave her a side eye. Okayyyyy then what are we doing.

We are going to feed our soul first and then we will feed our body.

She started lighting a candle in front of both of us and as I sat watching her every move, she asked me to repeat after her.

Shanti Mantra
Om Saha Naavavatu
Saha Nau Bhunaktu
Saha Veeryam Karavaavahai
Tejasvi Aavadheetamastu Maa Vidvishaavahai Om

I never did anything like this before, but I don't see anything wrong with it. I guess, so I repeated.

Shanti Mantra
Om Saha Naavavatu
Saha Nau Bhunaktu
Saha Veeryam Karavaavahai
Tejasvi Aavadheetamastu Maa Vidvishaavahai Om

I had to ask, Undyn what exactly are we doing and what am I saying.

She responds, this is meditation and in English translations it means...

May the Lord protect and bless us. May he nourish us, giving us strength to work together for the good of humanity May our learning be brilliant and purposeful. May we never turn against one another.

She then explains after we say the chant we sit still and free our minds and allow our hearts to expand. You will know when you are done because the spirits will guide you to your end.

This all really sounded weird to me, but I was still going with it. About one minute into this meditation, I began to feel extremely emotional, it was as if someone had opened the door to all of my pain and deep buried anger, then began pulling it out of me. Tears started to fall but I didn't let that break my meditation. I continued to breathe and the more I inhaled and exhaled the better I felt. It was as if a monk was sitting right next to me guiding my breathing.

This must be what she meant I thought. When I opened my eyes, I didn't realize but 15 minutes had passed and Undyn was right next to me extending her hands for me to grab. Just as I grabbed her hands, she pulled me in and gave me a hug that felt like the arms of God were embracing me himself. This was an amazing feeling. We sat for several more minutes and it was just what I needed. We ate the delicious meal she prepared and like she said we fed our soul and then our bodies. I was full on so many levels. This trip to India was life changing to say the least.

CHAPTER XIV.
ZEALOUS

Having or showing zeal.
"the council was extremely zealous in the application of the regulations"

W ow who would have ever known I would be graduating top of my class from air force boot camp. I was recommended to pilots' academy based on my exceptional performance. My dad was smiling with so much pride; I know I made him happy.

 I called Cat right before our hell week so I am sure she will be happy to hear the update as well. Last we spoke she was trying to tell me about someone she met that was supposed to be so amazing. We needed to finalize our vacation plans together since we both have free time in a couple of weeks. I wish I had more time to talk with her, but I had to report for formation check in on the yard.

With everything that's been going on I didn't get to tell her about Jerome, the guy I have become really close to. It's funny how some things come full circle. Who would have ever known that guy in high school that I bumped into while in a Japan would end up back around the country in the same boot camp as me. He in some ways reminds me of Cat with how big his heart is but then a little like my dad with how protective he is of me too, so I think I have the best of both worlds. The only catch is he was talking about some girl that he may or may not be married to and they may or may not have a kid. I really didn't think it would ever become anything between us but now that it has, I think maybe it's a good time to revisit those conversations especially since we will both be in pilot academy together.

Airman First Class Alexus Daniels...

Tech Sargent called my name to walk across another stage to receive my military diploma and awards but this time I made it look really good. If I don't do anything else good in my life, or if

I go to pilot school and fail miserably, this day will be something no one can take away from me. This just may be the proudest moments I have for myself. Way to go me!

CHAPTER XV. REUNIFY

Restore unity to (a place or group, especially a divided territory).
"Charlemagne's attempts to reunify Western Europe"

osta Rica here we come!!! I am so excited I can't wait. I thought getting a flight and approval was going to be much easier, but my parents still seem to think all things must run through them first. I have to admit I am looking forward to being on a beach with fresh smelling water. A nice change from India and Georgia; I have so much to tell Lexi.

Thank you for your service. Thank you for your service…

I really appreciate all of these people saying that, but I don't think they know I have not served anything except hard times in boot camp. Who knew walking through an airport would be so challenging. I don't know how celebrities do it. If I could, I would change out of this uniform and walk around like a regular civilian, but we were given strict orders not to do so until we arrived at our final destination. We represent our country at all times; call it a blessing and a curse. I have about 45 minutes to kill before my flight leaves I guess I can check in at the counter.

Thank you for your service, the airline attendee said. Would you like to be upgraded to first class? she asked.

Uhm; only if I don't have to pay for it I respond.

No, you don't have to pay anything extra. It's company policy to upgrade our military service men, and women, when space is available. Today, space is available, as she smiled.

Well of course! As if I had said no thanks lady. Heck yeah can I go now is what I was thinking.

Well, here you are… as she punched on a few keys and handed me my boarding pass back.

You are all set and again thank you for your service.

No thank you, I really appreciate it. On second hand, I don't think it's anyone's business that I haven't served anything yet. If it gets perks like this, I will listen to that line all day long. You are ALL very welcome!

Welcome to Costa Rica – the pilot said over the loudspeaker. We do hope you enjoyed your flight with us and will be happy to serve you on your return flight home. You are free to unbuckle your seat belts and enjoy your stay in Costa Rica.

CAT!!

LEXI!!!!

We run to each other like the scene from color purple, when Celie and Nettie reunite. We were so happy to see each other.

Cat, look at you, you look like a Bohemian, all grown up.

Look at you! You look so serious and official. I almost didn't recognize you in the uniform.

Hey, don't talk about the uniform; this baby got me a first class upgrade free of charge, thank you.

Are you serious?! All I got was peanuts and a ginger ale in coach. Talk about a bad flight. Not to mention the crying baby that kept kicking the back of my seat. Who cares, I'm just glad to see you.

We sat in the middle of the baggage claim area talking as if we were not going to be with each other for the next five days. We walked and talked and talked and walked. Good thing we had transportation vouchers to our resort so all we needed to do was look for the resort shuttle name instead of being harassed by taxi drivers trying to take advantage of silly tourist.

Tell me about Spellman and your trip to India.

As Cat begins to talk, I observed her whole being. Her body language was different, the way she spoke and how she seemed to carry this amazing confident energy I never felt from her before. She had a glow about her. While she is telling me the details of what she experienced from the food at school to the all-night study sessions in the student union building, not to mention the people and challenges of India it felt like she was leaving something out.

I don't know what she experienced but it's like she was born again. Her views about different people and life were different. She used to be so fragile, sheltered and timid, now she seems to be so confident, self-aware and fearless with an overwhelming sense of peace. I am looking at a newly transformed person and for some reason I feel so proud of her.

Now, enough about me. Tell me about boot camp and all the military madness. Is it like you see on TV or is it worse? she asked. Lexi start from the beginning.

I start with night one at boot camp all the way to graduation day. I made sure I didn't leave out the story about one of the guys who tried to commit suicide right after he failed hell week, as if he had nothing to live for after. At first, I felt like maybe the universe kept testing me, as if there was something I was supposed to know or do with witnessing stuff like that. But his time around I was strong enough to talk him out of pulling the trigger. I believe there was a stronger source that was guiding my words and energy that night but whatever it was made me a stronger person too. Cat listened to me just as I did her. We both gave updates on our love interest. Who would have ever known Cat would be the one to play on the other team.

Costa Rica was the most beautiful place I had ever been in my life. We saw waterfalls and walked through rain forest. Partied with the locals and made time to volunteer at a community shelter in town. Cat showed me how to meditate, and we did that a few times on the beach just as the sun was coming up. That alone was like connecting with the universe on another level. I'm glad I have that to take with me aside from these amazing memories that will last forever of this trip. I would say this was by far the best R&R we both had. I missed my best friend, but I am glad to know after all these years we still remain just that... Best friends.

CHAPTER XVI.
NOVELTY

The quality of being new, original, or unusual.
"the novelty of being a married woman wore off"

It's really interesting that everything I was taught about life, religion and self-worth was extremely limiting; and through my personal experiences I found that this huge world we live in holds more love, excitement and teachers than we give credit for. They say hindsight is 20/20 and I couldn't agree more.

Just because you go to a church more days than the average person, does not make you any more spiritual than a monk who spends hours in meditation on a mountain. Just because you have a degree in some special area of study does not make you any wiser than the man who grew up with a third-grade education but made a business selling his crops.

Just because you are married to the opposite sex with one child, does not make you any more valuable of a spouse or parent than the same sex couple who is married with two children by a surrogate. Just because your skin is lighter or darker than another does not mean you are entitled to any special treatment over the next.

Just because you were raised by two parents in a household does not guarantee you more love than that of a single parent. Just because the size pants you put on are smaller or larger than someone else does not mean you're any more beautiful.

I have even learned that just because you live in one country with many liberties and freedom of speech that too does not make you more liberated than those who live in third world communist countries considered to be poverty stricken. Just because a person whose scars are visually obvious does not make them any less painful than the one who was scared emotionally.

Just because a life was saved by a doctor on an operating table does not mean it is more valuable than the one that was spared from an attempt of suicide. Lastly just because your issues look one way in a package does not mean it's any less heavy; we all carry baggage that affects how we walk.

It is up to us to learn how we should carry it to optimize our journey that is called life. We are created in the divine image of our creator; we should honor the gift of life by living it fully and unrestricted. Curiosity doesn't always kill the cat; in my case it saved her.

THE END

ABOUT THE AUTHOR

Aundrea D. Veney

Aundrea Veney is a storyteller, mindfulness practitioner, and passionate advocate for trauma survivors. With a heart for healing through narrative, Aundrea weaves powerful, personal journeys into transformative stories that challenge norms and uplift identity. Curiosity Saves Cat is her debut novel, inviting readers to walk boldly into self-discovery.

www.ingramcontent.com/pod-product-compliance
Lightning Source LLC
Chambersburg PA
CBHW060651260626
47161CB00008B/3099